W9-ASR-850

E
RYA

Ryan, Pam Munoz.

Hello ocean.

C₁

$15.80   34880030024496

DATE			

BAKER & TAYLOR

HELLO OCEAN

HOLA MAR

Pam Muñoz Ryan ✦ Traducido por *Yanitzia Canetti* ✦ Ilustrado por *Mark Astrella*

TALEWINDS

A Charlesbridge Imprint

Hello, ocean,
my old best friend.

Hola, mar,
mi viejo amigo.

I'm here,
with the five of me, again!

*Aquí estoy otra vez
¡con mis cinco sentidos!*

I **see** the ocean,
gray, green, blue,
a chameleon
always changing hue.

*Yo **veo** las olas*
azules, verdes, grises
como un camaleón
que cambia de matices.

Amber seaweed,
speckled sand,

bubbly waves
that kiss the land,

Algas ambarinas,
arena amarilla,

olas espumosas
que besan la orilla,

wide open water
before my eyes,

ante mis ojos,
el mar ancho y bonito

reflected in a
bowl of skies,

*reflejado en el hondo
cielo infinito,*

glistening tide pools
and secret nooks—
I love the way
the ocean **looks**.

charcos brillantes,
escondites de coral:
*me encantan **las vistas***
que ofrece el mar.

I **hear** the ocean,
a lion's roar,
crashing rumors
toward the shore,

*Yo **escucho** el mar,*
rumor que estalla,
un fiero rugido
que llega a la playa,

water
shushing
and
rushing
in, then
whispering
back to
the sea
again.

murmullo de agua
que al llegar
susurra, y luego
regresa al mar.

Froggy songs from distant boats,
gentle clangs from bobbing floats,

el tenue sonido de barcos distantes,
el suave murmullo de boyas flotantes,

screak of gulls
calling down—

el graznido de gaviotas
que bajan a pescar:

I love the way
the ocean **sounds**.

*me encantan los **sonidos***
que tiene el mar.

I **touch** the ocean,
and the surf gives chase,
then wraps me in a wet embrace.

*Yo **toco** el mar,*
y el mar me enlaza,
con sus húmedas olas,
me envuelve y abraza.

Pulling,
pushing,
the restless sea
repeats the same
refrain to me.

Me hala,
me empuja,
el inquieto mar
repite lo mismo
sin descansar.

Waves that pounce
in rowdy play,

tide that tickles
with splashing spray,

*Las olas juguetonas
me golpean en la orilla,*

*la marea retozona
me hace cosquillas,*

squishy,   *tierra arcillosa*
sandy,   *fangosa*
soggy ground,   *arenosa*

slippery seaweed that wraps around,

cubierta por doquier de algas resbalosas,

sudden breezes
that make me squeal—
I love the way
the ocean **feels**.

brisas repentinas
que me hacen exclamar
¡Me encanta **sentir**
a mi amigo el mar!

I **smell** the ocean,
the fresh salt wind,
wafting lotions
from suntanned skin.

Yo **huelo** el mar,
*brisa fresca y salada,
lociones olorosas
sobre pieles bronceadas.*

Aromas from some ancient tale
disclose their news when I inhale.

Aromas que datan de antiguas historias,
y que al respirarlos traen nuevas glorias.

Reeky fish from waters deep,

Olores de peces emanan de lo hondo

fragrant ore from holes dug steep,

mineral fragante llega desde el fondo,

drying kelp
  and musty shells—
    I love the way
      the ocean **smells**.

  algas secas,
    conchas en mi collar:
      me encantan
        los olores
          que tiene el mar.

I **taste** the ocean
and wonder why
it tastes like tears
I sometimes cry.

*Yo **pruebo** el mar,*
y vuelvo a preguntar
por qué sabe a las lágrimas
que salen al llorar.

Sandy grains in a salty drink

Agua salada con granos arenosos

are best for fish and whales, I think.

para peces y ballenas es fabuloso.

I lick the drops
still on my face;
I love the way
the ocean **tastes**.

Las gotas en mi cara
me gusta probar:
me encantan
*los **sabores***
que tiene el mar.

The sun dips down;
it's time to go.
But I'll be back
to see your show,

El sol se oculta,
ya baja el telón
pero vendré de nuevo
para ver otra función,

hear the stories you have to spin,
taste your flavors once again,

oír esos cuentos que echas a rodar,
probar tus sabores una vez más,

take deep sniffs
of briny air,
and feel the treasures
you have to share.

Goodbye, ocean,
my old best friend. . . .

respirar profundo
ese aire salado,
y tocar los tesoros
que tienes guardados.

Adiós, querido mar,
mi viejo amigo. . . .

Para Nikki y Natalie Connor, simpáticas y complacientes modelos.
Y a las chicas que cumplen años: Sally, Kim, Barbara y Evelyn.

To Nikki and Natalie Connor, gracious and patient models, and to the birthday girls: Sally, Kim, Barbara, and Evelyn.

—P. M. R.

Para Alex y Joey, Allyssa y Ryan, Sean y Devon, Lauren, Phoebe y Jacob, Angel Mae y Maria Lanakila,
Susan D. y para cada chico que toma un creyón o un pincel ¡y hace un dibujo!

For Alex and Joey, Allyssa and Ryan, Sean and Devon, Lauren, Phoebe, and Jacob, Angel Mae and Maria Lanakila,
Susan D. and every kid who picks up a crayon or paintbrush and makes a picture!

—M. A.

© 2003 by Charlesbridge Publishing.
Translated by Yanitzia Canetti
Text copyright © 2001 by Pam Muñoz Ryan
Illustrations copyright © 2001 by Mark Astrella
All rights reserved, including the right of reproduction in whole
or in part in any form. Charlesbridge, Talewinds, and colophon
are registered trademarks of Charlesbridge Publishing, Inc.

Published by Charlesbridge
85 Main Street, Watertown, MA 02472
(617) 926-0329 • www.charlesbridge.com

Library of Congress Cataloging-in-Publication Data
Ryan, Pam Muñoz
   [Hello ocean! English & Spanish]
   Hello ocean = Hola mar / Pam Muñoz Ryan ; illustrated by
Mark Astrella ; translated by Yanitzia Canetti.
       p.   cm.
Summary: Using rhyming text, a child describes the wonder
of the ocean experienced through each of her five senses.
   ISBN 1-57091-372-2 (softcover)
[1. Ocean—Fiction. 2. Senses and sensation—Fiction. 3. Stories in
rhyme. 4. Spanish language materials—Bilingual.] I. Title: Hola
mar. II. Astrella, Mark, ill. III. Canetti, Yanitzia, 1967- IV. Title.
PZ74.3 .R93   2003
[E]—dc21   2002015634

Printed in South Korea
(sc) 10 9 8 7 6 5 4 3 2

Illustrations done in acrylics on airbrush paper
Display type and text type set in Goudy Oldstyle and Leawood
Color separations made by Sung In Printing, South Korea
Printed and bound by Sung In Printing, South Korea
Production supervision by Brian G. Walker
Designed by Paige Davis